ONCE IN A LIFETIME

Their Gaze, Her Love and the Black Swan

Margareth Moore

purposes only and are the owned by the owners themselves, not affiliated with this document.

Table of Contents

SHOWER GIRL

As in other parts of the country, I am on self-quarantine, everything that is of interest is closed until who knows when. I experienced the interruption of normal life first hand when I finally had to go shopping.

When I arrived at the grocery store, a small snake was waiting for me. Yes, they limited the number of customers in order to maintain social distance. The line moved pretty well, one out, one in. Luckily, people just got what they needed and went out again.

Once inside, I noticed a young woman from the gym, who usually works out on the elliptical machine in front of me. She usually comes in with her husband, a military man. I can't say that we really know each other; we may have spoken a few times over the year.

A week before the gym closed, I noticed that her husband was not with her. I asked about it, and she said that they had put him on for a while, so she would come alone for a while. About the only other thing I knew about her was that her name was Janene and that she was an elementary school teacher and not from this area. Not that I didn't want more information, but she didn't open up much.

Janene waved to me from the production department, I waved back as usual and continued shopping. She checked out in front of me and so surprised me by waiting for her outside. It is uncomfortable to maintain a safe social distance when you try to have a conversation, but she started talking.

"Bob, can you help me since you know my husband has been deployed and I'm here all alone?

"Sure, Janene," she thought she needed help with the shopping bags.

"Bob, I really need a place to shower, my apartment complex is having water problems. The manager can't seem to get a plumber to fix it. First the hot water went, then all the water stopped, it can work for a few minutes and then stop. I almost got a cold shower, but the water stopped while I was soaped up, and when it was running again, it was brown water".

"I don't know any plumbers, I don't know how to help."

"Could I come to your house and take a shower?"

Janene is a young, attractive, thin woman with a nice, firm butt, at least from my point of view at the gym. I'd like to help her, but immediately I hear my wife's voice in my head saying, "No way.

After a long pause: "Okay, I'm sure my wife won't mind.

As soon as these words came out, I knew that I had committed myself to something that my wife would object to.

"Janene, give me your phone number, I'll text you our address."

Chapter Two

Later that day she called: "Bob, the situation is even worse now, I have to leave my apartment because several tenants tested positive for the virus. I'm scared... what am I gonna do?"

"What do you mean you have to leave, are you infected?"

"No, but several of my neighbours have tested positive and are now in quarantine. My husband suggested I go away for a while to be safe."

"Did he suggest a place where I might go?"

"No, I can't go back home because my parents' place was quarantined and I can't go where my husband was stationed. Please help me, I don't know anyone else in this area I could ask."

"Okay, we have a guest room, you can come over."

"Thank you very much, I bring my own shopping and I have my own toilet paper."

My wife almost blew up when I told her that she needs more than a shower, she has to stay for a short time until her apartment complex is repaired. I hesitated to mention that several of her neighbours had tested positive for the virus, but for our own health I had to mention it. I played down the health risks, but my wife said she would call her friend who was a nurse to get advice.

Her diabolical Angelia is a dental hygienist, not a nurse, but I would not stir the pot.

"Angelia said we can contact a doctor, she knows it, and he can do a telemedicine video check to examine your friend.

"Carol, I called the doctor to figure out how to do this safely. He told me your guest should take off all his clothes and leave them outside in a plastic garbage bag. She should go straight into the shower, shower with bacterial soap if you have it, and then contact me for a telemedical examination. If she passes the health check, she'll be safe with you. You should wash her clothes with a small amount of bleach to kill any germs before she can use them.

That one arrived at the front door, I told her to use the garage entrance. I printed out the doctor's instructions and taped them to the inside garage door.

She knocked on the inner garage door, "Bob, you can't be serious about these instructions, I can't do this

"Janene, this is Bob's wife, Carol. These instructions are from a doctor, we don't want to get infected with the virus. If you don't follow these instructions, you cannot stay here. I'm sorry."

A few minutes later, she knocks on the door: "Okay, I'm undressed, can I come in?"

"Can I come in?" "Anything? Including your underwear and shoes?"

"Yes, I'm standing here completely naked."

"Okay, I open the door, go straight down the hall to the bathroom on the right. It's all there, special antibacterial soap and towel. When you're done, come into the living room and we'll contact the doctor."

"Carol, Bob's not gonna see me naked, is he?"

"Janene, I sent Bob to his office in the back room, he won't see you."

Carol opened the door and got out of the way so Janene could go right into the shower. Then she sprayed Lysol on the door handle and took the garbage bag with Janene's clothes and put them in the washing machine. She wanted to separate everything, but she remembered that it was about disinfecting.

Janene was done and went back to the living room with a towel wrapped around her as ordered. The towel was not big enough to cover her top and bottom at the same time. She decided to cover her breasts.

Carol reached out her hand, but then remembered the new greeting: "Hi, I'm Carol. Sorry for the extreme precautions, but doctor's orders."

"Thanks Carol, I know this is an imposition but I have no choice and I'm scared to death. Especially since my husband is on God knows where."

"Janene, we'll call the doctor and do your telemedical examination so we can both calm down."

Carol tried to get the telemedicine doctor on her iPad, but couldn't get the connection. In her desperation she had to call me to help: "Bob, I can't get this damn iPad to work, can you help?

I entered the living room and noticed that both Janene and Carol were tapping the iPad everywhere, a total violation of the virus protocols. "Hey, ladies, step back, I'll do it after I wipe the screen with an alcohol swab."

I typed in the number, and the doctor was on-screen live in seconds. Dressed in a white lab coat and a face mask, he certainly looked like he was following proper protocol.

"Hello, I'm Doctor John Hopkins. I assume the woman with the towel is the patient. Please let her get closer to the iPad so I can get a better look." I'm speaking in an Indian accent.

Janene moved closer to the iPad to please the doctor.

"Thanks, I need to take your vitals, Carol, do you have that thermometer I requested?"

"Yes, doctor and I have the pulse ox and BP you requested."

We have a number of medical devices left over from years of taking care of Carol's father.

"First, Carol puts on examination gloves, then she takes her blood pressure and puts the pulse oxymeter on her index finger.

"BP 120/65 and pulse ox 98."

"Good, good... Take her anal temp now."

"Janene, bend over so I can take your temperature."

"Whoa, wait a minute, you're not sticking that up my ass!"

"Janene, this is the best way to get an accurate temperature. One of the first symptoms of the virus is an elevated temperature." Said the doctor.

Janene gave way and bent over the living room chair, her pale white butt exposed.

Just as Carol was about to insert the thermometer, the doctor's voice told me to hold the iPad so he could see her butt. Then she told Janene to spread her ass cheeks with her hands to make it easier for Carol to insert the thermometer.

That asshole croaked in anticipation of the foreign body being inserted. Not only was her ass visible, but her labia were also visible.

After an initial gasp, Jenes ass accepted the thermometer. The doctor warned Carol to leave it in for a full two minutes.

"98.4, Doctor," shouted Carol as she tried to take the temperature.

"Okay, that's good. Janene, we're gonna have to start at the top and examine you further. Carol, can you take a tongue depressor and look down her throat? Bob, can you move the iPad so I can see, can you put a flashlight in it so I can see better?

"Okay, well... I don't see any inflammation. Janene, I need you to remove the towel now so we can do a breast exam."

"Breast exam? What do my breasts have to do with a virus?"

"The virus can have many symptoms and can lie dormant in several places. If fluid is leaking from your breasts, it can be an early indicator. If fluid leaks, we can take a sample and have it analysed.

Janene looked confused. "I think that's fine, but does Bob have to see my breasts?

"I understand Janene, but Bob has to hold the iPad while Carol examines your nipples. Bob will keep his eyes closed if that helps."

After Janene has removed the towel from her breasts, "Carol, you need to palpate her areolas. If you feel anything unusual, stop so I can see."

Carol palpated them carefully and found nothing to report.

"Next, you pull on her nipples as if you were trying to milk them and look for signs of fluid leakage. If there's a stop and you take a sample, we can have the lab analyze it. Bob, I need you to move the iPad closer so I can get a close-up of her nipples.

I thanked the doctor and moved closer to Janene's nipples. I watched them harden as Carol pulled and twisted them; I think she became aroused. She didn't notice that I hadn't closed my eyes.

This went on for several minutes, I think Carol enjoyed playing with her nipples and could have gone on like this for longer, but the doctor said that was enough as there was no fluid.

"Last step Janene, I have to do a pelvic exam. There could be signs in your vagina. Sit in the chair, then I want you to move your labia apart and Carol will use a tongue pusher to hold your labia majora open so I can see your cervix. Bob, shine a flashlight in here so I can get a clear view."

As she removed the towel, her blonde pubic hair was cut off in a small, clean triangle that ended just above her pussy. I expected her to object to this further penetration of her body, but she agreed to it for fear of contamination.

Imagine this: My wife has a tongue depressor in a strange woman's pussy while I'm holding an iPad and a flashlight shines in her. Never in a million years did I think something like that would happen.

"Carol, move the handle to the right... "now to the left... Now I want you to pull back the clitoral hood, the little flap of skin where the inner lips meet."

Janene gasped as Carol uncovered the clitoris, and when she touched it with the tongue depressor, she pushed her hips forward and moaned.

Carol immediately stopped thinking she had hurt her, "Sorry, I didn't mean to hurt you."

The doctor threw in: "Yes, hmm ... the clitoris is swelling up ... that's a good sign. Okay, um... all done. I see no signs of a virus."

We all sighed with relief before the doctor continued: "Anyway, you should take your temperature in the next two days, just a precaution. If her temperature gets above 99, call me back."

Together we thanked the doctor and ended the iPad session.

Janene looks at Carol: "Now you know me inside and out."

"I'm sorry we had to put you through this examination, but the doctor said it was for all our safety."

Janene said, "I guess there's no hurry to put my clothes on now, I have no secrets now.

"Janene, when you're sitting on the furniture, please sit on the towel." Carol said casually, as if it were normal to say something like that.

A naked Janene went to the panoramic window of the living room and shocked Carol as she stood naked in plain view, watching the neighbor.

"Janene, would you like a tour of the house?"

She accepted, and Carol led her through each room, including the guest room, until she reached the rear covered patio. Janene, was admiring Carol's flower garden as the flowers appeared. Absent-mindedly, Carol suggested that Janene go outside and take a closer look, forgetting that she was naked.

"Wow, the sun feels so good" as she stood in the backyard.

"Carol, you should try this, being naked outside feels so free and natural.

Carol didn't answer. Carol just stared at Janene's young, slender, naked body as she walked around her backyard.

When they finally got back to Carol, Carol yelled, "Bob, can you put Janene's laundry in the dryer, I forgot all about it.

I expected Janene to ask if her suitcase was still in the garage so she could have clothes, but she seemed content to stay naked. Later, Carol suggested that I spray her suitcase with Lysol and take it to the guest room.

Carol surprised me with her reaction to Janene running around naked. I thought she had a problem with me looking at a strange naked young woman, but I think she enjoyed seeing her in that way herself.

"Carol, I hope you don't mind, but I think I'll go to the guest room and lie down for a while.

Carol took the opportunity to have a private conversation with me in the kitchen: "Bob, did this doctor look familiar to you?

"Familiar as who? ... we don't know anybody with an Indian accent, let alone a doctor."

"I thought it strange that he called you by name. You didn't tell him your name."

"My Skype ID is bob32, maybe that's why."

"I also thought it was weird when he went for a pelvic exam and the nipple exam was a bit suspicious. Not that I didn't mind, but it seemed weird." Said Carol with a raised eyebrow.

"Well, you had to admit he was thorough, and I'm now very confident about her health, and it was for our safety.

Later that night at the diner, Janene appeared in a light-colored gown that barely covered her nakedness.

"Carol, I'm sorry to cause you all this trouble and thank you for getting a doctor to examine me. I didn't want to bring germs."

"You're welcome. It's the least we can do for you."

Janene's bathrobe kept opening up, giving me a look at her tits. Carol chose this time to ask about her apparent lack of embarrassment with nudity.

"Carol, I love being naked, when I'm at home I don't wear clothes, I like the freedom of being naked. If I could, I would go to the gym naked. I'm not ashamed of my body, but I could stand to lose a few pounds.

"Well, we don't have a problem with you being naked, do we, Bob?"

I could only nod affirmatively for fear of choking on my mouth full of food.

When they cleared the table, I went to the garage to make a phone call.

"Carl, or should I say Dr John? What were you doing? I just wanted you to take her temperature and give her an okay."

"Bob, I couldn't resist when I saw the body. I wanted to explore it in every detail. You can't tell me you didn't want to see those tits. I just wish I could have made a house call."

"Carol would have made you in a heartbeat. She was still suspicious, but she left thinking you were a real doctor. She'll kill you if she ever finds out."

In his Indian accent, "What do you doubt about Dr. John?"

"Best April Fool's joke ever, pal, but Angelia's gonna castrate you if she finds out you took advantage of a young girl at her best friend's house."

"Good point, I won't tell anyone about this, neither can you, or Carol will castrate you too."

When I got back, Carol said, "Bob, who did you call?"

"Just a friend from the bowling league."

"You know, Bob, I've been thinking about the telemedicine doctor and Jane's checkup. I think I should let him examine me, just to be sure."

"Do you have any symptoms?"

"No, but he's had such a thorough examination, but I want to be sure. He should examine you, too, after you've done so much shopping."

THE POLICE HARRASSMENT

I'd gone to the library to return some books to my mother. When I walk home, I can go through a small, clean alley, which cuts my walking distance in half. So here I was trotting down the alley when three men came into the alley from the other end. When I talk about men, I suppose they were about my age, eighteen. I knew they were, if I remembered that we all had birthdays in the same month.

Now I was white and a girl and they were black and men, but was I worried? Certainly not. The three of them were very nice, and I had been in class with them at different times. I assumed it would be just a case of just saying "hullo" and passing each other and continuing on our way. It was not to be.

Even before we reached each other, this policeman stepped into the alley behind the men. He slammed his nightstick hard against a fence and yelled at the boys.

"All right, you scumbags," he yelled. "Stand by the fence and take up your positions and don't even think about running. I'm armed and perfectly willing to shoot."

I saw the consternation in the men's faces and the irritation when they saw that if they tried to run they would have to knock me down. They used highly inappropriate language as they turned and leaned against the fence, their weight on their hands and their legs spread. There was now a second policeman, and the two policemen moved towards the men.

I was outraged. Really angry. The boys had done nothing, they had just walked by and minded their own business, and the policemen had gone after them for no reason.

"Why are you picking on them?" I said. "You didn't do anything wrong. There is no law that says you can't walk in the street. That's harassment."

The three men looked at me in surprise, and then one of them smiled.

"Hey, Celia," he shouted. "How you doing? You tell them, girl. We ain't done nothing, and this is police harassment."

"Please go on, mademoiselle," growled one of the policemen. "This is a police matter and I would be grateful if you would not interfere."

"This is a police matter and I would be grateful if you would not interfere." "This is a nuisance to honest citizens. It's also racial harassment."

"Miss, we have a reason to stop these men," said the policeman. "Please let us perform our duties and move on."

"The reason, Celia, is because we are black," shouted the man who called me earlier. "As you can see, there are four people on this trail, and they only caught the three black people."

"He's right," I said in a righteous rage. I can't stand racism and injustice, and this seemed like a classic example. "If you are so faithful to your duty, why didn't you make me take the position you so originally called it?

The two policemen looked at each other and seemed slightly annoyed. Then the policeman who had been talking the whole time shrugged.

"If that's what you want," he said. "Assume the position." He nodded towards the fence.

"What?" he said. That was a joke, wasn't it?

"Assume the position. You've convinced me that I have to check you out too, to prove we're not acting from a racial profiling position."

I'd said too much to back down now. I turned around and put my hands against the fence.

"Not like that," the policeman grabbed. "Take a step back and lean into your hands. Spread your legs wider apart, too. The position is such that you cannot turn against the policeman. If you even try, we can kick your feet out from under you before you can take action."

Oh, so that's why they did it this way.

The other cop started frisking the man at the end (is that the right word).

"Bingo," he said, holding something up. Next thing I know, he's handcuffing the poor man.

"I'll just put him in the car and be right back," he said.

After a minute he came back and started to check out number two. "Bingo two," he said, and another set of handcuffs was made and the man was led away.

The first policeman started to check the last man while I tried to turn around to see what he was doing. His hand came out of the man's pocket with what looked like a pair of necklaces.

"I think I got bingo too," he said with a grin, and number three was handcuffed.

"You can run them in," he said to his partner. "I'm staying with the young lady until the policewoman arrives."

I was pretty nervous now.

"What's going on here?" I asked.

"Three men have just robbed the jewellery store," said the policeman. "We had a pretty good description of them, so we stopped the three men. Guess what we found in their pockets."

I didn't have to guess. I'd seen what he'd pulled out of the man's pocket. The three of them were probably laughing morbidly at how gullible I'd been.

"I did not know. I didn "t know. I "m sorry. I feel like a fool. Can I go now?"

"Ah, I'm sorry, but no. Now that we have due process of law, we have to go by the book. You must be searched. Don't worry, I won't search them. My partner will send a policewoman to take care of it."

Oh great, I was going to let a strange woman feel me up.

"Oh. Uh, how long will it take her to get here."

"I don't know. They're only considered part of due process of law and not high priority. She'll turn up when she does, but don't worry. She shouldn't take more than an hour or so."

An hour or so, with me leaning against that fence the whole time? You gotta be kidding me.

"Oh, come on," I moaned. "You can't expect me to stay here for an hour or so."

"Hey, don't blame me. I told you to keep moving. You're the one who insisted on butting in."

"But I didn't know."

"Did you think to ask or was it just more fun to accuse the police of the wrong thing?"

It made me blush. He was right. I liked having an excuse to yell at 'em cos I knew they wouldn't do anything. Taking that position was something I hadn't expected.

"Can't you just go through my pockets or something?" I begged them.

"Hello. Me Tarzan, you Jane. What do you think of that?"

"What?"

"The police will only search suspects of the same sex.

"What, no exceptions?"

"Only if the suspect voluntarily agrees to be searched by a member of the opposite sex. Men often volunteer, women almost never."

"But they can? They can do a quick search, if I agree?"

"I could, but I'd rather not. "Women can change their minds at any time and complain later. Why should I risk it if I can take it easy for an hour or so?"

"Oh, come on. That is so unfair.

"OK, fine," the policeman grumbled. "Anything to shut you up. But don't whine to me if it makes you uncomfortable."

He advanced behind me and ran his hands along my sides and under my arms. Then his hands went around the front of me and began to stroke my breasts. I began to blush with embarrassment, but my blush jumped in full bloom when he stopped and pressed a finger on a nipple.

"What do you have in your pocket?" he asked.

"I have no pockets on my blouse," I said in a rather hoarse voice.

"Oh, right," he said, apparently realizing what he had pressed. He laughed softly, I just knew it.

He crouched behind me and his hands closed over one of my ankles. Then he rose again, his hand running up both sides of my leg. I blushed, but I honestly expected him to stop as soon as he reached my skirt, or maybe just to the bottom of my skirt. His hands just kept going up, and I gasped strangled as his hand bumped against the crotch of my panties and pressed firmly against what was on the other side of the crotch.

Did he apologize? In your dreams. He just crouched down again and his hands brushed against my other leg. He won't have to climb that high this time, I kept telling myself, because he had already looked there. Did that stop him? The hand that was pressing against my pussy told me no.

"Almost done", he said, as his hands slid over my hips, still under my skirt, mind you.

When his hands came down, my panties came down with them. One hand pushed my panties down further while his other hand started rubbing my pussy.

"What are you doing?" I was half screaming.

"I'm just making sure the last part of the search goes smoothly for you," he said.

"What are you talking about?"

"You wouldn't believe where a woman hid a switchblade yesterday," he told me. "That is why we must be very careful and very thorough in our searches. Don't worry. I can handle it."

Maybe he could, but could I? That was a very personal part of me that he wanted to search.

"Ah, maybe we should wait for the policewoman," I said, and even for me my voice sounded a little rough.

"Don't be a sissy," he mocked me gently. "I'm almost finished. Just relax and we're done."

I still said, "But," as he spread my lips and pushed his nightstick into me. And I meant his personal baton, and it felt thicker and harder and much hotter than his silly little police baton.

I said, "You can't" and "You shouldn't" and "Someone might come" and his baton kept pressing deeper and deeper. In retrospect, I guess I should have said things like "no" and "stop." Those words are so much more meaningful than insinuations that maybe this was not a good idea.

He didn't even bother to slow down, he just pushed hard until he was completely embedded in me.

"Yes", he breathed gently into my ear. "I can pretty much guarantee that you have nothing more to hide up here."

"So that means you're gonna take it out now?" I asked hopefully.

I heard a faint giggle, his warm breath blowing against my ear.

"Wouldn't it be a waste of a good start to take it out now?" he asked. "Why don't we just let things go on as they are for a while?"

Look. This is what happens when you ask questions instead of making statements. People answer the questions wrong. He started to move and slide back and forth and stir me up. To my surprise, I realized that even in the position I was in, I was able to answer and move with him. Even more to my surprise, I realized that this is what I wanted.

Slowly but surely he moved in faster and faster. At the same time my enthusiasm grew at the same pace. I gasped for breath, pressed myself urgently against him, wanted to have this cock deep inside me and enjoyed the feeling that he was rubbing against me.

The only fear I had now was the fear that he might stop before I wanted him to. I begged him, urged him to get harder, asked him not to stop. Everything piled up inside of me, stressing me, and I almost screamed, just because I knew we were outside. My former fear that someone else might come was forgotten, but that did not mean that I wanted to attract them. I just didn't want him to stop.

He gave me one last push, and I went out of the deep, trembling as my climax broke into me, and felt him moaning and writhing and shaking as he himself reached the climax.

He pulled himself away from me, we were both breathing heavily.

"I must admit that you are quite clear about me," he said. "You are free to leave."

"Thank you', I said, wondering at the same time what I wanted to thank him for.

"Just remember that in general we have a reason to stop people and racism is not one of them. If we arrest somebody for racism, we will probably be sued, and we cannot go on patrol when we take cases to court.

So I drove on my way home, chastised accordingly. I decided that I didn't like to accept this position as the police described it. It seemed to have left me with very shaky legs.

THE DOCTOR'S VISIT

It's not all sexy. But sometimes, just sometimes, you smile and go with a swagger.

Patient S. Abdominal pain. 26. F.

She was fine after surgery. But we had to monitor her for the next two days. I was on call in the post-op ward. I was just doing my post-op observation. There were four patients in this room. Miss S had just finished her meal when I consulted her chart. The usual greeting. She leaned over, squirted some hand sanitizer and rubbed her hands together.

"No, no, no, no." I said. "You must wash your hands properly. Come to the washbasin, I'll show you."

She looked a little perplexed and nodded. Pulled the sheet back and threw her legs out of the bed. The bright red nails of her toes and slender legs caught my attention. She stood up. During her night she wore a thin cotton nightgown that barely covered the tips of her thighs and was strewn with small yellow flowers. Strong breasts held the nightdress out and let it cascade over her figure. She was short, perhaps 1.2 m tall, and had long brown hair on her shoulder blades. I had to control myself to see her face. She was pretty. She gave me a sweet smile, questioning eyes, beautiful blue-grey eyes.

She went to the pool. I stood beside her and slightly behind her.

"First the soap, rub it over your hands, between your fingers, wrists, everywhere," I said as she continued to rub the greenish liquid over her delicate hands.

"Here, like this." I walked behind her and put my hands on hers.

There's something special about hands touching. No, not the way they shake hands, but the touch of the fingers touching fingers, hand on hand. As if it were a personal caress of the heart. When my hands touched hers, when I reached for her from behind, she felt it too. Her head turned upwards and looked at me with those big eyes, her mouth was slightly open.

"Let me help you," I said as my fingers slipped between hers. She spread her fingers apart and allowed me intimate access to her hands. Her skin was so soft and my own hands eclipsed hers. As I stroked her hands, I gently turned her palm upwards, my hands sliding over her palms and back between her fingers. I could hear her breathing in. I felt her body relax. I moved a little closer, my head lowered to just beside her. I could smell her hair.

"Just like this." I almost said in a whisper. "Back and forth. Back and forth between the fingers." As I spoke, I felt her body gently press into me, her neck twisting slightly as if it were an invitation.

"You have beautiful hands, Doc," she said. She turned her head, looked me in the eye and smiled.

"Thank you. Now we must wash up." I bent over to press the washstand, as I did with my own torso pressed tighter into her. I became quite aroused. Her hands were so small, so soft, and her fingers were so pleasant to feel.

Whether she felt my growing hardness, she did not say. I was sure that she could, for her body was now pressed against me. I continued to wash her hands thoroughly. I had to go away and get her a paper towel to dry.

Then she jumped back into bed.

"Much better, all nice and clean." I said.

"Doc, I have some complaints," she suddenly said.

"Oh, let me have a look." My concern for her after her operation. There could be complications. "Can you lift your gown for me so I can look?"

She reached under the sheet, pulled the hem up under her breasts. Wow, her nipples were hard. How could I have missed her before? Then she rolled down the sheet to expose her stomach. I put my hand there, two fingers squeezing in pieces to measure the pain.

"Is it uncomfortable here?" I asked.

"No. None. Actually, it's a little deeper." She said her hand rests on mine. Then she held my hand and slipped it under the sheet. I felt the soft fluff of her pubic hair, the rise of her mons pubis. Her hand kept moving mine. I heard my own breathing change. Her breath became loud and deep. She moaned very softly with my hand between her legs. Her hand on top of mine moved her up and down.

"I think she needs more attention." I breathed. I slipped my middle finger between her smooth labia. I felt the exquisite texture of her smooth skin, her inner flesh. It felt moist and warm, the delicate creases on both sides of my finger as I stroked it up and down. Her breathing and moaning was more serious. She began to lift her body from the bed, began to bend her hips and arch her back.

"God, Doc, that feels so good," she whispered. She looked at me with desire.

As her bloom opened for me, I pushed a second finger to allow me further access. Now all my fingers, my hand lovingly stroked her wet pussy in a constant rhythm. She moaned again. The heel of my palm stroked her clitoris, my fingertips searched for her entrance and inserted two while I spread my fingers apart. Now I fingered seriously and searched for her excitement until the climax.

Her breath was so deep. I could see the oven in her eyes. Her hand reached out to my ass and squeezed it hard.

"Oh, yeah, damn," she moaned. "Right there, damn." Her voice crackled with delight. Her body almost writhed under me.

"Oh fuck, oh God, I'm coming..." She almost moans a whimper. I could see and feel her trembling. Her body cramped up against my fingers deep inside her. "Oh, mmmm." The words escaped her lips as she closed her eyes and enjoyed the feeling. My hand slowed and had to stop as she squeezed her thighs.

I felt her tremble for a few more seconds before she let go of me. My hand went over her mons pubis and out of the sheets. I looked at my fingers whose tips were covered with milky juice. I put them in my mouth, sucked and licked her sperm and tasted her very sexy pussy juice.

"Thank's Doc. That feels so much better." She said. Her voice almost giggled.

"Well, I'm very well-behaved at my bedside, they tell me." I answered.

She giggled, such a sweet, sexy giggle.

"I'll come back in an hour and check on you." I said.

"Make sure you do. I think I might have a sore throat when you get back," I kept her hint as my cock popped into my pants.

And so it happened. An hour later she was sucking my dick. The next hour we fucked. She's being discharged today, someone else's shift. I'm gonna miss my patient. I just hope she still knows how to wash her hands.

MYSTERY ON THE LOWSIDE

Vasquez sat in the SUV and painted her nails red. She didn't like the color much, but it was such a slow day that she decided to paint them. After lunch she repainted her nails with white tips.

She liked the change she was in, but the novelty had long since gone. The local sheriff had given his county a reputation for keeping most troublemakers away, so she had little to do.

"Cart four, cart four!" the radio yelled, scaring Vasquez.

"Car four here, move over!" She barked at the radio.

"We have reports of a fat man pushing a motorcycle down Custer Road." The radio said. "You've got to see this."

Vasquez sighed, and when she got calls, it was always about silly things.

"Car four confirmed." She told me to put my hand back down.

Vasquez looked in the rearview mirror to check her makeup and hair. She was wearing her shoulder-length brown hair loose under the standard issue Stetson hat she was wearing.

"You're fucking sexy!" She explained throwing the gear selector into the drive.

When she arrived on the scene, she saw a man pushing a motorcycle by the side of the road, but he wasn't as fat as the reports said.

He was more out of shape than chubby, he was wearing a denim jacket with his arms exposed, Vasquez gasped when she saw how muscular those arms were. He had a thick brown beard and hair, which was best described as... as untamed.

"Where are you going?" Vasquez said out the window to the man.

The man kept pushing his bicycle, Vasquez almost thought he didn't hear them, then he spoke up.

"Third star to the left..." The rugged man said, without looking at her. "Then continue until dawn."

Vasquez laughed at this grown Peter Pan; he was as smart as he was mean, and she liked that. She pushed the gas to pull ahead of him, then cut him off and stopped to get out.

"Do you have a name?" she asked.

She asked, "Yes." He answered with a grim look.

Vasquez knew the guy, she kept silent until he spoke.

"They call me Guardrail." He grunted, and then he hit her in the eye and asked. "You have a name... Officer?"

When their eyes met, Vasquez felt a sensation she hadn't felt in a long time. It wasn't love or physical attraction... She was attracted to him, but it felt more like a spell. Whatever it was, she knew she had felt it before.

"Um..." She said, regaining her senses, "They call me Maria Lara Rodriguez Enojado Vasquez."

"Uh... right." The brute replied.

"Everyone calls me Vasquez." She said with a smile. "Well, how can we help you today?"

The biker seemed happy about it, though he wasn't smiling, but his frown seemed less sinister to Vasquez.

"I need gas, a place to sleep and some tools, I need to fix my bike," he said.

Vasquez opened her mouth and said she had a gas can and directions to a mechanic who could accommodate him for the night, but what she said instead surprised her.

"At the next intersection, keep right and keep going until you see the house with the RV in front of it, my place is next to it. I can rent you a room while you work with your bike?" she said.

"Sure." He said as if that was the only answer he could have expected.

Vasquez got back in her SUV, then made the sign of the cross. As she drove off to find a pendant for his bike, she mumbled the Saints' names in her ear. Although she was incredulous, she did exactly what he asked her to do.

An hour later she had Guardrail's bicycle in her garage and he was standing with her in her living room.

"Would you like some water, maybe a bite to eat?" She kept asking and asking herself how this man got into her house.

"No." He said if he thought about it, he said, "Get me a beer."

"Madre Dios!" She freaked out when she walked into the kitchen. "I gotta get back to work, the sheriff's gonna be mad!"

Guardrail opened his drink, then stood there staring at her while he pondered her words. She assumed that the Sheriff, who had attacked a man during the second battle of Fallujah, might have had a good reputation.

"Do you have time for a quick one?" he asked and took a sip of beer so big that he spilled his beard.

"No!" said Vasquez and turned his back on the biker.

She imagined herself getting into her SUV and then driving away, but to her own amazement she began to loosen her belt.

The biker laughed at his good luck, Vasquez was initially terrified as she pulled down her pants. She was quickly replaced by curiosity, she was not very horny, she wanted to know why she bent over a sofa.

"Do you have a rubber?" she asked, pointing at the biker with her naked ass.

"Ha!", was his gruff answer.

Vasquez heard his pants fall to the floor, followed by his heavy kicks towards her. She knew the Sheriff would be pissed off that she was wasting so much time running around and getting laid.

Her anticipation grew until he finally touched her, expecting something rough, like a slap or being pushed down. But he grabbed her Stetson hat!

His touch was not gentle, he tried to pull her top up, but with her bulletproof vest and bra he had no success.

"Shit!" he said in frustration.

Now it was Vasquez's turn to laugh.

She heard him spit into his hand, something she'd always been disgusted with. She was a woman who got wet quickly and easily, getting ready to fuck was never a problem. If those strange days came when she wasn't wet, she was ready to suck cock first.

When he pressed against her, she felt her body being pushed into the air. She did not feel well at all!

"Hijo de puta!!" She screamed: "Uh... that's my ass."

The guardrail grunted again and then slid down. This was always a moment of anticipation for Vasquez, often suggesting whether a man would be great or terrible.

She hadn't had a look at his penis, but when he pressed his head into her, followed by his shaft, she knew he was about average in size and length. Vasquez really wanted a black cock, but she was content to enjoy what he had to offer.

Oddly enough, she could tell he had foreskin. She felt the ribbed sensation that the extra flesh flap gave her. She could also hear Guardrail moaning with pleasure as he pushed himself deeper.

Though it was the strangest sexual encounter of her life, Vasquez couldn't help but notice when she arrived. What Guardrail lacked in foreplay, he made up for in thrusting. The sound of the wet slaps as their bodies collided was soon drowned out by the sound of her moaning.

She took a deep breath and filled her lungs, during sex all her senses came to life. This time she could smell many things mixed together, including his beer breath, gasoline and his body odor. It was obvious that this road traveller had not enjoyed a shower for some time.

Vasquez could feel the motorcyclist's fleshy hands pressing closer to her hips. She could also feel his growing orgasm as his grunt grew deeper and more guttural. In the past, she had let men cum quickly, but they had always kissed her first.

"Shit, you're tight!" he explained in a low tone of voice.

"Maybe it's not so bad," Vasquez thought as she smiled at the compliment.

Without warning, the man behind her quickly raised his hands along her body. She wasn't worried that if he wanted to get in trouble, he could have done so earlier.

He lifted her shirt and slid his hands underneath. Vasquez knew exactly what the heavy-built stranger in the denim vest wanted.

"They're all the same," she thought as his hands raised the underwire of her bra.

Now it was her turn to grunt as he slipped his hands into a bra that barely held her twins away. Normally she would take off her bulletproof vest and then open her bra, but this time she was content to grab the arm of the sofa.

Guardrail didn't have the biggest cock she had experienced, but his hard knocks were certainly unforgettable. The roughness he showed to her nipples was unlike any other partner she had recently.

"Uhnnnnnn..." Vasquez moaned as she came a second time.

His blows were now even fiercer and more powerful, Vasquez knowing the end was near. His grunting was louder than before, his hands squeezing her breasts even tighter.

Vasquez felt her orgasm brewing in her loins, she did not want to be cheated by this dirty biker! She pushed her hips backwards to match his forward stomping.

"Uuuuugggghhhhhh!!" Guardrail grunted as he came into her.

"Madre Dios!!" yelled Vasquez as she came too.

She felt his sperm penetrate her, it was a heavy, thick load. She assumed he'd been on the road so long he didn't have time to put the old stuff away.

Since care was not an issue for Guardrail, he took a few steps back and then pulled up his pants. Vasquez could hear him breathing heavily.

She placed a pair of pants over her crotch because she didn't want a massive

pile of semen to land on her service pants. With her pants back on, she turned around and saw Guardrail yawning and turning around as if he was trying to find something.

"What's wrong?" Vasquez asked the lost biker.

"Sleeping." was the caveman-like response.

"Lie down on the sofa." She said, "Fix her clothes. "I have to get back to work."

The Neanderthal who had banged her just before shuffled zombie-like in Vasquez's bedroom. She felt the strongest urge to pull out her service weapon to give him an extra bellybutton, a quick glance at a watch convinced her otherwise.

"¡Llego tarde! ¡Mierda! ¡Mierda!" she cried out as she ran to the door, her Peter Pan of a playmate snoring in her bed before she left the driveway.

Later, back at her speed trap, her phone rang.

"¡Mierda!" Vasquez snapped when she saw it was the sheriff.

She slipped in her seat uncomfortably.

"Hola!" she said, trying to sound happy.

"Hola-shmola!" cried the sheriff in a deep voice. "Tell your new friend to get the fuck out of my county!"

Vasquez sat back down in her seat as the Sheriff kept screaming. The Sheriff's words had not only scared her off, but she was sure that the load of semen the Guardrail was carrying inside her was beginning to run out of her!

"His bike needs fixing." She remembered what the biker had told her before.

"Yeah, he's got three days, then I'm getting a warrant to search his pig!" The sheriff droned.

Vasquez opened her mouth in response, but the Sheriff had already hung up. She was angry, but also very curious about the bike.

SPEED TRAP

The night was so humid that your shirt would be soaking wet within 10 minutes if you were outside. The deputy of the local county sheriff was sitting in his favourite speed trap. He was sweating like a whore in church.

He knew he'd catch a couple of speeders here as usual. But for some reason, this night was slow. A car hadn't passed by for over 30 minutes. When he sat down at his personal cell phone, he went through his pictures. He had stored a few of them that he had taken of a girl he had fucked a few weeks ago. She had big tits that he liked to pinch and bite. Hitting her made him hard.

Her ass was big, and when she bent perfectly round, he beat it good until it turned red. She loved him, too. It made her squeal and moan. He also spanked her fat pussy lips. It really turned him on and her on too, so she had to beg him to fuck her now!

When he thinks about it, he looks at the picture of her legs, how she spreads her pussy lips open and makes him rub his hard cock.

Giggling, he hopes that no car with his angry boner bulging in his tight uniform has driven in the meantime. But don't you know, a car speeds by. His radar showed it at 60. That was a 45 mile an hour zone.

The top of the car was down because he saw that she was cute.

So he slammed his car into the road and he raced after her. And he still had one hand on his hard cock. After he caught up with her and ran over her badge, he hit his headlights and then the siren in two short bursts.

Her music is so loud and she sings the song on the radio so intensely that she doesn't realize that she is being stopped. When she hits a sign, she sees blue reflected lights hitting the sign. She looks in her rearview mirror.

She takes her foot off the gas and slows down a little. When she hits the brakes, she stops on an old dirt road that looks like it hasn't been used for years. Weeds and grass grew wild in the middle and on the lanes.

She drove on for about a minute, moving far away from the main road so that they could not be seen by other passing motorists.

This was her intention, as she had done in the past, to get out of a parking ticket.

When she sat down, she wore a nice, tight mini skirt that reached close to her crotch and almost showed her panties. The top she was wearing was thin, almost transparent, with long, thin straps over the shoulders. Her big bouncing tits pulled on the weak straps and showed so much cleavage and tits that she might as well have been topless. When she saw this, she pulled them even further down, almost showing her brushless, hard erect nipples. Then she wiggled her seat enough to reveal her panties.

The officer gets out of his car and goes to the driver's door of her car. He hopes that she doesn't see half his erection.

Ma'am, I'm gonna need to see your license and registration, please.

Sure, officer, just one second.

He sees the tits almost popping out of her top. Then he sees her panties reaching for her purse in the passenger seat. His dick is fully erect again.

Ma'm, do you know how fast you were going?

No, sir, how fast?

60 mph, that's a 45 mph zone.

As she hands him her license and registration, she looks him intensely in the eyes and asks, "Is there anything I can do to make this go away", while she slowly pulls her top down, showing all her tits. She winks at him and looks at his cock and sees his erection. As she reaches down she pulls up her skirt and shows her pussy hill in her white lace panties rubbing her finger on her clitoris in circular movements.

The officer knows that there will be no ticket in this case. He can't help it, she was too fucking hot!

She had long black straight hair that reached up to her big sexy ass. Beautiful big brown eyes. Beautiful face and tits that stood straight out, firm without bra.

Ma'm, please get out of the car.

She opens her door and gets up in front of him. She is taller than him in her high heels in high heels. Her tits still exposed, she pulls her skirt further up and reveals her softly tanned belly.

Ma'm, turn around and put your hands on the car, please.

She does what she's told, bending over a little more than necessary and stretching her ass towards him as if to tell him: Here it is.

He starts to frisk her from the ankles. He rubs her tanned legs to feel how soft they are, but they were tinted. He slowly works his way up to her ass, which shows both ass cheeks, because she is wearing a lace thong. He rubs her ass cheeks and squeezes them together with his hand, feeling the tanned flesh between his fingers. He slaps her pretty hard. She moans. He slaps the other one, she moans more. He reaches around her and feels her big tits. Damn, that was the best one so far, he thought. He had stopped a few times with these results, but this was the best looking one ever.

Yes, he was weak when it came to beautiful women, but what could he do? He's just a man. He's gonna fuck him real hard. And maybe it won't be the last.

He'll pinch her nipples real hard to make her squeal. He plays rough with them while he rubs his throbbing cock against her ass as he bends over her.

He tells her to turn around and squat down.

She does as she is told and grabs his zipper, pulls it down and then pulls out his throbbing cock. She licks her lips and takes her head into her hot, wet, soft mouth. No sooner does she suck on it than she tastes his foreplay, which oozes out whatever irritates him. He grabs both hands full of her beautiful black hair and moves her head closer, pushing his cock deeper into her mouth. He watches her gagging and takes everything.

Looks like you've done enough of that to know how to handle it. Suck that cock good for Daddy. Suck me dry, bitch!

The dirty talk only made her wetter and she sucked it harder. She fingers her clit and pussy with one hand while holding his dick with the other. When she looked up to him with her beautiful brown eyes, he pushed it harder and harder into her with her beautiful brown eyes and pressed her head with his hairy hands equally to counter his thrusts.

Yeah, you sucked a lot of cocks, didn't you, you little slut?

That's it baby, suck daddy's dick mmmmm fuck yeah suck it harder, I'm gonna cum all over you!

He stops her by pulling back her head and pulling out his wet cock dripping from her saliva.

He grabs her by the waist and lifts her onto the hood of her car, not caring if he's still hot from the engine. He makes her burn those luscious ass cheeks. Something for her to remember him by.

She doesn't care if the hood is hot or not. At this point, she could care less. He grabs her ankles, pushes her legs up and leans down and buries his face in her wet pussy. Damn, she smelled and tasted so good. His face was wet from her juices literally dripping from her hot pussy. He was eagerly licking it up. He started sucking on her clit, nibbling on it and sticking two fingers up her pussy and a third up her ass. She moaned loudly and wiggled her pussy on his face. Oh, daddy!! Right there!!! Suck my pussy, OMG!! He sucked her clit hard so it would come off. She moaned loudly, it echoed through the night, but nobody heard it, at least not a person. Her body shook with lust. She fucks his mouth and rubs her juices all over him while she hums.

He pulled her off the car, turned her around and pushed his cock through her pussy lips from her clitoris to her ass back and forth until she begged him to fuck her and fuck her hard. He slaps her ass cheeks alternately with each stroke. Her ass is red. He loves it!

He slaps his dick hard. He's pounding it in as hard as he can. He grunts because it feels so fucking good. He's fucking her hard and deep with every stroke so she screams and squeals. He spreads her ass cheeks wide so he can try to get in deeper.

He can feel his sperm boiling. He bangs one last time and empties his load into her as much as he can. He moans and grabs her fleshy ass cheeks and makes them redder. He lies down on her and takes a deep breath. Damn, should he have sperm in her? What if she's not using birth control? Well, she was nice and hot. She'd be even prettier if she was carrying his baby.

THE COP

It's one of those days, and I need to blow off some steam.

I get upset when I hear the siren. I sigh and look for a place to stop.

The policeman walks to the car. I roll down the window. He is amazingly handsome, with sand-blond hair, dark stubble and a strong jaw. He wears mirrored airplanes even though it's dawning.

"Good evening, miss," he paints. "I stopped you tonight to inform you that your taillight is broken. I will give you a work order to get it repaired."

"Thank you, I had no idea." I'll give him my license and registration. "I'll take care of it right away.

He goes back to his car. I look at him in my side mirror and I watch his ass as he walks away. I put my lipstick back on.

He comes back. His fat forearms bend as he hands me my papers back.

"Here you are, miss, you're ready."

"Are you sure you want nothing more from me?" I slowly lift up my skirt to reveal my white cotton panties. I caress the fabric. "Is there anything else you need from me?"

His empty expression remains motionless.

"Don't miss, you can go", he says aloud.

He turns off his body camera, goes to his cruiser and returns with more force in his step.

"Get out of the vehicle," he barks.

"Yes, officer."

I stand seductively and make sure he gets a good look at my legs. We're on a small country road with nothing but farmland as far as the eye can see.

"Turn around and put your hands on the vehicle. No sudden movements."

I obey. The policeman pats me down and roughly pats every part of me. He moves his palms along my legs and between my thighs. I open myself up for him and he probes my pussy with two fingers. A car drives by. He slides his little finger up my asshole and my knees go weak.

He drives up north and takes off my blouse. He puts his hands under my breasts and squeezes my tits. He uses his body to push me against the door. His erection is pressing on my ass.

He ties my hands behind my back and turns me over so we're facing each other. He slaps me. Hard. I gasp from the shock and the pain.

"Are you ready for what comes next?"

"Punish me," I moan.

"Get on your knees."

The cop unzips his pants and unfolds his smooth, trimmed dick.

I kneel in the gravel and take it in my mouth. I lick his frenulum and massage his head with my tongue. I taste old sperm at the tip.

It's hard to keep my balance with my hands behind my back. I almost fall into him and he presses me on his cock with both hands. He fucks me viciously in the mouth and I hear another car driving by, this one slower.

"Shit!" He pulls out his dick, and I try to catch my breath. He pulls me by my ponytail. "Get up."

He throws me on the passenger side of his cruiser and pushes me down so

I'm out of sight. He tapes my mouth shut, and we pull away and leave my car on the side of the road.

When we arrive at the old factory, it is already dark. We're about thirty miles out of town, and not a soul in sight.

The policeman cuts off the engine in the middle of the parking lot. The entire property is damaged by age and neglect. The motion-activated floodlights are so bright that I feel like I'm at a high school soccer game.

He pulls me out of the car and opens the door to the back seat. He pushes my face into the shabby upholstery. I'm ready for him.

He lifts up my skirt and roughly pulls off my underwear. He spits on my pussy, but I'm already wet. He rams his cock in and fucks me hard and furious. I scream to the gag and I press my ass into him while he takes me from behind. He pulls me back by my hair and with one hand he covers my throat. When he climaxes, he pushes my face into the seat and he slams my naked ass together.

The cop pulls me up like a rag doll and marches me to the wire fence. He takes off my handcuffs, only to have my hands zipped up in front of me. I raise my hands above my head and he ties them to the fence with another cable tie. I drip with anticipation.

He steps back and looks at me. I blink into the bright lights. He's a shadow, a silhouette.

He unbuttons my blouse, thin and white with red dots. I wear a wide white skirt, espadrille wedges and a white and gold cross around my neck. He pinches my nipples together until they are hard. He slaps me again and I fall back into the fence.

A set of headlights turns into the parking lot. It's another police car, then three more.

They're standing in a group talking, but I can't hear them. Occasionally they shoot at me and look at me. Then they stare at me openly. I turn around and grab the fence and push my ass out so they can take me in completely.

They walk towards me with strong, deliberate steps. I can't see their faces, only darkness. I spread my legs and lean on what is about to happen.

The first policeman smokes a cigarette on the hood of his car and watches the other four take turns with me. He does not say a word.

The second policeman seems ashamed and can't look me in the eye. After a few minutes he ejaculates.

The third cop is a show-off and fucks me like a porn star. He lifts me up by my hips and pushes into me while I hold on to the fence. He sucks my nipples through the wafer-thin fabric. He plays with my clitoris and hits my G-spot at the same time. I can say that he enjoys the audience.

The fourth cop is rough, almost too rough. He pulls down my skirt and whips me with his belt until my ass is red and piercing and covered with welts. He twitches my hair, slaps my tits and rips my bralette to shreds. He caresses me with his baton and knocks the chain link inches away from my body. He holds my throat with both hands while he fucks me to the end.

The fifth cop is friendlier. He peels the tape back and kisses me. I wrap my legs around his ass and crunch into him while the shackles carry my weight. I come to a climax and my screams echo.

They take turns with me for the next hour. No one speaks. My body aches and semen drips down my thighs. The glue of the tape burns my lips. My wrists are red from the stiff plastic bands. I come, over and over again.

One by one they all drive off, until only me and the first cop are left. I hang limply from the fence. My body is buzzing with excitement. He buttons my shirt, adjusts my clothes and puts my hair back in place. He slips into my shoes and ties the ribbons together with a bow.

"Let's get you to your car, miss."

He cuts the zipper that ties me to the fence, but leaves the others in place. I'm still gagged. He helps me into the back seat and ties my ankles with duct tape. All I see is the roof of the car and the mesh cage that separates us.

Somebody's crackling in over the radio. We drive off into the night.

IN DEPTH INTERROGATION

In the dim light emitted by the only 60 W bulb dangling from the ceiling, her breath stirred the fine particles like dandelion seeds blown by a summer wind from the Midwest.

"...which I want you to answer as truthfully as possible. And although I cannot advise you ..." her voice went in and out as his mind followed random, incoherent thoughts. Words piled up like tree trunks that piled up in a stream, disordered and chaotic. Locked in this room, his thoughts disappeared from the walls and collided with hers. The serious tone with which she spoke referred to a circumstance as alien as the place where he was.

"Okay, so let's start slowly: Please tell me your name. Can you do that?", she asked pedantically.

After a long pause he spoke. "You already know my name. Next question," he said with a hint of anger.

"Listen, I'm trying to help you, Joey, if you could just play along, that would be great!" she flattered him.

"I am Joseph Randall, at your service," he said with false glee.

"Good boy, Joey. Now we're getting somewhere," she said as she turned around in her chair, loosened her long, muscular legs and crossed in the opposite direction. The smile on her face confirmed her deviant intention in this subtle act. "Well, do you know why you're here?"

"I don't know because I don't go to church," he offered.

"If you want me to help you, you have to stop this shit. They're making some pretty serious accusations against you," she said with sincere concern.

"What do you want from me?" he exclaimed.

"I want to know if what they say is true," she demanded.

"Well, then ask," he replied.

"It says here that you have requested various deviant sexual acts from an honourable woman," she explained.

"Requested? That's a lot of crap. I have written poems and other rubbish that no one should read," he said.

"Yes, well, someone read them," she assured him. "And these 'poems', as you call them, could be seen as a threat of violence," she explained as she looked up from her notepad, took off her glasses and put one of her arms in her mouth while she thought about what she would say next. "I must say that some of the things you have written are worrying.

"Like what?" he asked.

"You wrote, and I quote, 'I'm going to nail your arms and legs down, put my body on top of yours and remind you what it feels like to have the weight of a man on top of you,'" she said and her voice softened when she finished.

He offered a grin as the only answer.

"'I will grab your face and force you to look me in the eye as I move your body back and forth, subjecting your body to my will', she read. "That sounds like a threat, don't you think?"

"It's fantasy. I didn't threaten anyone,' he explained.

"Is it 'sticking your cock down her throat' before she can say any part of that fantasy?

"Okay, taken out of context it sounds terrible," he admitted.

"So in what context would you 'shove your cock down someone's throat' and it wouldn't be an act of violence?" she asked cautiously. Her voice was curious and her body bent inward when she asked.

"This is a fantasy. Some people like that,' he said.

"'Some people'?' she asked. "Would these people like it too... ... "um, let's see," she said as she turned over her notes. "Do they look into your eyes as they slowly take the full circumference of your cock in their mouths?"

"I think so," he said defensively.

"Has anyone ever done this for you, Joseph?" she asked.

"No. At least not yet," he said.

"And you think that the threat of holding someone will inspire him to do that?" she asked incredulously.

He sat there in silence and raised his shoulders as if to say, "I don't know.

She got up from her chair and walked around the table to which his hands were handcuffed. As she stood behind him, she grabbed the back of his chair and turned him to the side. Although his hands and feet were bound in fetters, his body was now turned to the side. Very clumsily she reached down and unbuckled his belt, his button and his zipper. "Let's see what kind of belt we're working with here," she said mockingly.

As she unzipped his trousers and pulled down his panties, she exposed his flaccid penis. As she reached into his pants, she pulled out his balls and cock for examination. "There's not much strap here, Joey," she joked. "Not sure if it would reach down to the neck, Big Shooter," she said with a laugh.

When she touched him, he started to swell up. Within fifteen seconds, he was completely erect. After watching him grow, she stood back for a moment to think. "Okay, well, this could make a difference."

On her knees, she knelt down and looked up at him after carefully inspecting his fully erect dick. "So you expect someone to put the whole thing in their mouth?" she asked, while her head was lowered. The heat of her wet tongue on the head of his cock was like an electric shock. She flicked her tongue all the way along the edge and probed briefly before accepting the head through her lips.

The saliva from her mouth covered the tip and upper part of the shaft of his cock. She stroked with her hands and spat out some of her saliva. She began to descend on his tail, taking an extra millimeter each time she descended.

"Is this what you were hoping for?" she asked sarcastically.

"I was hoping that she - or I guess you now - would go further," he said cautiously.

"Uh, I don't know how you expect me to put any more of this in my mouth," she said with a smile.

"Try again," he said and returned her smile.

As she lowered her head again, he moved his elbow over the back of her head as she put the tip in her mouth. His arm squeezed gently as she came down. When he allowed her to come up again, he pushed her head a little further down the next time and then a little further each time in succession.

As she pulled back, she looked up at him. "I'm gonna gag if you keep this up. Is that what you want?" she asked.

"Hold your breath and try again," he said with a nod.

She followed his suggestion and took a deep breath before taking his throbbing tail in her mouth. She felt the head of his cock crash into the back of her mouth and press against the opening of her throat, causing her mouth to salivate. Bouncing up and down, slowly overcoming the gag reflex, she absorbed more and more of him.

When she stood up, she wiped her mouth and picked up her clipboard again. He gave a deep sigh of frustration. "It says here that you also had fantasies of watching her undress?" she said as she began to unbutton her blouse. Within a minute she had thrown her blouse and skirt on the floor.

"And then it says here that you wanted to lean back when she sat on you?" she asked. "You wanted her to grab your cock and stick it up her hot, wet pussy?"

She spoke as she moved towards him, lifting one leg above his lap and spreading it. She grabbed his cock and looked into his eyes as she maneuvered his cock so that it floated between her dripping wet labia. "Is that what you meant?" she asked as she lowered herself onto him.

"Yes", he replied.

"And you wanted to feel her turning on you, her tits flying around in your face? Did you want to slap her? You wanted to feel her up? Squeeze her?" Her voice trembled as the pleasure began to take over. "Suck them. Suck her, Joe. Suck my tits, Joe. Bite them a little. Bite me, Joe. That's what you want, huh? Bite my nipples, Joe. "Shit, Joe," she said while she was out of breath.

"And then you wanted her... feel her..." Her voice faded as she approached her climax. "Pussy dripping on your dick and balls?"

She rocked back and forth, hard against it, up and down and in a circular motion. "Oh fuck", she screamed as she started to come. Her body twisted on top of him for another 30 seconds as she exhaled her explosive orgasm.

Standing, out of breath, she walked over, picked up her clothes and sat back down on her chair. After a few minutes of labored breathing, she was now back in her clothes and her notepad in front of her again. She was barely able to control the broad smile.

"So this is what you write about," she finally asked.

"Only you left out the part where, after you come, you get down on your knees and finish me..."

PULLED OVER BY A COP

Flashing lights become visible when you look in your rearview mirror. A pit forms in your stomach when you notice that a policeman is standing directly behind you, the lights flash and signal you to stop. Nervously you look at your speedometer, which shows 78 MPH. You slow down as you use the indicator. Slowly you come to a halt at the side of the road. You see the lights of the police car parked behind you. At night, it's almost blinding. While you think about the consequences, you ask yourself how much the ticket will cost, how much your insurance will increase? You wait for what seems like an eternity while the policeman remains in his car.

You start thinking of a way to get out of a ticket. What if you could come up with an excuse? Would he understand if you just told him the truth, that you were on that empty road late at night and that you didn't notice how fast you were driving. Maybe you could find a way out if you had the courage to flirt with him. How far could you let yourself go? When you think about the possibilities, you feel a familiar tingling sensation rush through your body. You feel a wetness growing in your pussy.

A tap on the window snaps you back to reality. When you become aware of the situation again, you shuffle in your seat to adjust your legs, a futile attempt to deal with the itching that began. You look dazed at the flashlight shining through the window as you roll it down.

"Do you know why I stopped you, miss?" You look up at him to answer and realize how cute the officer is. "Uh, I, uh..."

"Miss, have you been drinking tonight?"

"No, sir, I'm just a little tired and nervous."

"May I see your driver's licence?" You nod and explain that it's in your purse on the passenger side. He turns on his flashlight to see the handbag and asks you to take it. You unbuckle your seat belt and reach for the handbag while the light falls on it. You bend over and feel your shirt slide up your legs, knowing that your ass controls are almost exposed and the light is suddenly redirected. You begin to wonder if he's looking at your ass. You sit back and hand him your license. He shines his light on the ID. You look down at your legs to see how far up your dress has slipped, and you see that some of the light is shining directly at your exposed pussy. You now wish you had worn panties, but this exposure excites you even more. You start to wonder if he's doing it on purpose, you feel the wetness between your legs growing again. You rub your thighs together and let out a slight groan as a sharp feeling of pleasure runs up your body.

"Are you all right, miss?" You nod, "Why don't you get out of the car for me?" He reverses as you open the door. His light flashes on you as you swing one leg out of the car. He turns the light down when you try to get up. Again, you realize that your pussy is displayed for his eyes as you get out of the car.

"Why don't you lean against the hood of your car?" As you follow this and lean your ass lightly on the hood, you think again of miracles. You start fantasizing that he actually looked at your pussy.

Instinctively, you start rubbing your thighs together again and feel your skirt rise. A light flashes on your face and pulls you out of your fantasy. "Miss, get up and turn around. I'm going to check you for drugs or weapons. Do you have anything on you?"

"He instructs you to put your hands on the hood, spread your legs and relax. As his hands begin to rest on your back, they move to your breasts and cupping them while you let out a moan. Then he moves down your stomach and pulls you up against his crotch. You wonder if he did this on purpose and if you felt his hard cock or if it was something else. It was quick and then he moves his hands over your ass, suddenly you feel your skirt being pulled up. You wonder if he did it on purpose and his hands reach around your inner thighs. His fingers lightly stroke your pussy lips. You let out a steady moan of the loader.

"What was that lady? Are you all right?" You didn't answer me. You're not sure where this is going, but your silence will encourage him to decide where it will lead. Suddenly he'll pull your arms around your back and gently press your upper body against the hood. As he holds your hands together, he asks again, "Miss, you have been acting strangely, are you drunk or on drugs?

In panic, you say "No".

"Then why are you acting so strange?"

Without thinking, "Because I'm horny, my pussy's wet, and I need it touched so bad right now. When you realize what you just admitted, you wonder what's gonna happen next. Then a smooth, hard object runs down your pussy lips. Your legs shake while you expect to get what you want. As that object slides back and forth across your pussy, he asks, "Is this what you want, bitch? Do you like it when my nightstick rubs against your pussy?" Then it lightly taps the inside of your thighs, indicating that you should spread your legs wider. He pushes the end of the nightstick against your pussy. He lets go of your hands. "Do you want that inside you? Then bring it in."

They reach between your legs and guide the hard stick inwards. He pushes it in slowly as he turns it, covering the nightstick with your juices. He fucks you slowly by pulling it out and pushing it in. You pick up the pace as you breathe heavily and moan loudly and start rubbing your clitoris.

As you cum, you scream and your body presses against the hood of the car. Your legs are the only thing keeping your body from slipping. The nightstick slides out leaving an empty space, but is suddenly filled again when the policeman shoves his cock inside you. Your weakened legs begin to give way as his hand presses your body harder against the hood. You regain strength and push your body off the hood to counter his blows. He pulls at your hair and guides your body so that it presses firmly against his. His hands surround your breasts and massage them through the light material.

He pulls himself out to your disappointment. He turns you around and lets you sit on the hood. He lifts your legs over his shoulders and leads his cock back into your waiting hole. While your pussy is being fucked fast and hard, you move your hand back to your clitoris while the other one rubs your hard nipples.

You get an orgasm again and you moan. You feel your pussy winding around his cock, he stops and pulls it out. He releases your legs and lets your body slowly slide down the hood. He brings your weakened body down so that you sit on the bumper. The orgasm still affects your body, his hand grabs your face and turns you towards his cock. You open up and he pushes his cock, covered with your pussy juice, into your mouth. You are already breathing heavily, you do your best to suck him while he fucks your throat.

Easily recovering, you take his cock in your hand for the second time and stroke the smooth shaft while opening your inviting mouth. Your tongue massages the underside of his cock while your lips run up and down tightly.

He moans and you feel his sperm build up, ready to explode. Your hand, wrapped around his head with your tight lips, twitches his cock up and down, milking him of his sperm. A hot jet squirts into the back of your throat, then another one and another one. You try to keep his sperm in your mouth, but as his cock empties between your lips, something drips down your chin and onto your dress. He closes his cock back in his pants while you watch, collects the remaining sperm around your lips and swallows it.

You stand up and wait to see what comes next.

"Now, miss, I advise you not to drive horny again if it makes you go too fast. Hopefully we'll have fixed the problem by tonight. You should be able to drive now. Drive carefully."

You're sitting in your car starting the engine when the policeman drives away. You managed to get fucked and not get a ticket. Now you hope that your husband won't notice the sperm stain on your dress if you get home later than expected.

THE COP'S OFFER

I was in the heat of summer in a fallow field waiting for a buyer that I thought would be late. When I saw the team car on the dirt road, I knew it was a set-up.

It was not a well-planned operation, as there was a fast-moving irrigation canal less than 10 steps away from where I was. When the policeman arrived where I was standing, we both knew the evidence was gone. I had thrown it into the canal as soon as I saw it. By then the powder was gone, and he knew it. But that didn't stop him from arresting me. He was mad.

He was rude and made a very thorough search, even though there was no female office. He seemed terribly enthusiastic to check that I had nothing hidden in my bra. He also checked my lower level quite well - it wasn't the third base - but only a small piece of cloth away. I was not really surprised. When he tried to get on my nerves, he had no idea what kind of life I had led at home.

When I was sitting in the back seat of his car in the summer heat of over 100 degrees, the nice officer decided to have a chat. This was not a new tactic either. I was allowed to sit in the back in the oppressively hot air of the car while he stood outside and talked to me through the half-shattered windscreen. I was ready for the questions and for the heat. If that was all he had for me, I would have been all right.

The questions were so predictable. Where did I get that from? And what was it? How much did I sell it for? Did I know what the punishment was for selling drugs near the high school? Why didn't I have any ID on me? Charged questions you'd be stupid to answer, and no matter what my Miranda rights were. This was a small town, and they did things their own way.

I lost my ID, had no idea what he was talking about, and I was in that field because I had to pee. Playing dumb is easy and I was good at it.

Eventually, however, the conversation changed its course. The nice officer wanted me to know that he knew me and everything about me. He asked me by name about my boyfriend. It was hard to say that I didn't know Ronnie - we had lived together - but I just pretended not to know anything that was true in many ways.

When I didn't give in, he became insulting and asked me what it was like to use tricks at the rest stop. (I had done this, but not in a long time, because it didn't pay off well - but I had been put away for hooking before, and we both knew it). He asked me how much I was charging and if I was going to take it in the ass. I didn't take the bait and just ignored the questions. One of Ronnie's lawyers had driven this into my head.

Finally he decided to get personal - and took after my mother and father. It was a stupid move on his part. He had no idea what a monster my parents had been. But it got interesting.

"I was sorry to hear your daddy died," he said.

I'm sure he wasn't. No one in town liked my dad. His job as a payroll clerk at the local packing plant had made him an incredibly unpopular man. He was the guy who delivered the layoff slips and cut your pay if you were late, and he was an asshole to boot.

And the cop said, "Well, that's just as well. It must have been hell being married to that bitch."

I'm sure he was right about that part.

As I listened from the back seat of the police car, this policeman told me something I had suspected for years - my mother had never been completely faithful to my father. I had been mentally divorced from them for so long that it shouldn't have bothered me, but hearing the details was disturbing.

It turned out that my mother got around a lot - and her reputation was well known. She preferred uniforms - policemen, firemen and soldiers when they came through town.

She loved to ride in cars in the fields, but was even wilder when they jumped into a motel room.

She would not go home with any of them - not if they were married anyway. (She had her standards - she would not have sex in another woman's bed).

He also shared certain positions. "She likes to be on top, you know," he told me. "She probably didn't learn to sit on your daddy's face instead of his cock until after you and your sister were born, but she told me once that it was the only time old Roy actually used that mouth except to kiss his bosses' ass.

He wouldn't stop while I was roasting in the car. He talked shit about my mother. Finally, after describing in detail what kind of underwear she was wearing under her work clothes and how she probably "got hit on the chin" in the back seat of that police car, he contacted me.

If the other part had been unpleasant and my situation in the back seat hadn't been a little bit of hell, it would have been quick.

He told me they had been watching me and my friends, and at some point we would all "soon have our wings clipped". He told me that Ronnie had been in trouble before - which I knew - but that he had an amazing lawyer, which wouldn't matter this time.

"If we get him this time, everything will be by the book and airtight."

Then he started the trial.

"Will you like prison?" he asked. "Eat some carpet - be a lesbian's bitch? You think they're gonna love you in there? The lesbians will, but the blacks will stick a knife up your ass just because you're pretty." He added, "You'll be dead before your sentence is up. Probably about 20 years earlier."

Then I got the pitch - they told me there was one. They'd want me to testify as a key witness and rat on my friends, and if I did, they'd give me a light sentence. That was the usual pitch. This was gonna be a fishing expedition for the cops trying to gather evidence.

But it wasn't. Instead, I have something much easier to miss.

"You want protection? I can give it to you. Me and my friends at the station."

Then he opened the door to the back seat. Which was a good thing, because I was about to pass out from lack of air.

"You see, your mama's getting old and her tits sagging. We thought you could take her place."

So he unzipped his fly and pulled himself out. It was pretty obvious that he liked to think back to his wild times with my mother. I think he expected me to open up right away and pick him up - his dick was so close to my face I could have spit on it and hit the hole.

Just the thought of it was repulsive to me. He was older, heavy guy, a cop, and if you believed him, he he fucked my mother. What could be less attractive?

It wasn't my first rodeo, though. When your hands are handcuffed behind you and you're in the middle of a deserted field, it's not the right time to say anything provocative. At least you'll end up resisting arrest. At worst, you'll be buried under a cornfield, probably after being fucked in the ass and strangled.

I just kept quiet and waited.

At some point, even though no words were spoken, he understood the message. His dick withered in the heat and I think he understood that I wouldn't help him - at least not voluntarily.

He gave me a few words of encouragement, telling me that the policeman's tail was the key to my freedom. I wouldn't be asked to bend in any direction that Ronnie wouldn't have bent me, and there might even be some money or a hiding place for me in it. I sensed that he had given this speech before - and I didn't believe a word of it anyway. If I relied on the men in blue to keep me free, I would be on my knees and elbows the whole time, and we both knew it.

At some point I felt his unease about how to proceed and said, "Do you intend to rape me? Because if not, maybe

op." It was a phrase I'd used before with men
a little too brash. Usually I would talk some
to them, but his cold look scared me. It was as if
s thinking about it, so I made him a peace offering.

.l tell you what, I know Brenda has support at the truck
stop. Go to her and tell her that if she treats you well, I'll
slip her something later to make her feel good.

Brenda was a hooker who worked for the truck drivers
and she had told me about how she sucked a lot of cop
dicks to avoid going to jail. I'd seen her more than once in
the back seat of this cop car of assholes, so I assumed he
liked the service.

Eventually he put his dick away, but not before I noted
the size, shape and distinguishing features. (You never
knew when something like that might come in handy.)
He pulled out a cigarette, which he smoked with slow
fury.

He frowned and asked me why he wasn't as good as all
the truckers I had blown. He said he would only fuck me
in the mouth anyway and maybe he would try other
parts of me, but somehow I felt that his heart was not in
it. It turned him on forcing women into submission, I
could see that.

At some point he gave me the signal to turn around. He
took off my handcuffs and let me know that it was not

over yet and that I would be quite sorry that I had
swallowed my pride and his cock when I had the chance

Because of the drugs I had to throw into the canal, I
walked away about 300 dollars less. Even more
devastating was the way that the cop had peeled away
my dignity. I wanted to kill him for that.

Brenda told me later that day that he had been a very bad
man for her and I had to get her pain pills so she could sit
down. I did, and I was silently grateful that it was her
and not me.

I stayed as far away from him as possible and for a long
time he never got close enough to catch me doing
anything else, but then we were all hit hard. It was more
than a year later. Ronnie was still in prison, and the trial
wasn't even over.

I woke up in a hospital after an overdose. He was there,
grinning like a fucking Cheshire cat. I was handcuffed to
the side rails of the bed. I could see he had a hard-on just
looking at him. By then it was too late to negotiate.

not

Lightning Source UK Ltd.
Milton Keynes UK
UKHW022016190421
382278UK00003B/627